Beatrice Marean

An Original Drama in Six Acts

Beatrice Marean

An Original Drama in Six Acts

ISBN/EAN: 9783337376253

Printed in Europe, USA, Canada, Australia, Japan

Cover: Foto ©Andreas Hilbeck / pixelio.de

More available books at **www.hansebooks.com**

Beatrice Marean

An Original Drama in Six Acts

ISBN/EAN: 9783337376253

Printed in Europe, USA, Canada, Australia, Japan

Cover: Foto ©Andreas Hilbeck / pixelio.de

More available books at **www.hansebooks.com**

AN ORIGINAL DRAMA

In Six Acts, Entitled

CHERRY, or Labor vs. Capital.

——:o:——

BY BEATRICE MAREAN.

——:o:——

Written in Compliment to the
Greensboro Fire Department.

——:o:——

Respectfully Dedicated to the

Eagle Hose Company, No. 7,

Greensboro, N. C.

——:o:——

CASTE OF CHARACTERS.

CHERRY, a carpenter's daughter, in love with Rudolph Dean—a millionaire's son,. . . . . . LILLIAN BRADLEY.

JENNIE GOODWIN, Mark Goodwin's wife, ... Susie Brown.

MRS. DEAN, a rich widow—mother of Rudolph Dean, ... Marie Bancroft.

FLOSSIE MAXWELL, very rich, whose mother died when she was a baby, a diamond in the rough, . . Daphne Harding.

MARK GOODWIN, Captain of the Eagle Hose Co., No. 7, ... Harper Johnston.

RUDOLPH DEAN, a rich young man— madly in love with Cherry, . . John Lafayette.

CHARLIE HILTON, a loyal fireman—a member of the Eagles, ... David Walter.

UNCLE BOB, a wealthy western ranche owner,. . . . . Fred Newton.

BILLY OLIVER, a bicycle sport—who loves Flossie,. . . . . Claude Melnotte.

DENNIS O'FLANIGAN, a jovial Irish fireman, ... Clarence Barden.

JO BLACK, a tramp—rescued from a building, ... Edwin Clarke.

TWO POLICEMEN, in uniform, } . . . William Scott. } . . Arthur Jordan.

JOHN WILLIAMS, }   { Robt. Whiting.
JIM TRACY,   } Loyal firemen { Billy Adams.
FRANK WELLS, }   { John Wesley.

Members EAGLE HOSE COMPANY in uniform.

SYNOPSIS OF THE PLAY.

ACT I.—Home of Mark Goodwin. The serpent in the garden. Mark's denunciation of capital. The arrival of Uncle Bob and Flossie Maxwell.

ACT II.—The firemen's pic-nic. The secret meeting. Flossie's discovery. The promise, "I swear before the Almighty God, I will murder him."

ACT III.—The attempted elopement. Billy Oliver asks for Flossie. Uncle Bob's answer. The murder. Mark's return. "I arrest you for the murder of Rudolph Dean."

ACT IV.—The Engine House. The Eagle boys stand by their Captain. The fire alarm. The rescue of the tramp.

ACT V.—The trial. The conviction. The sentence. The tramp's confession. Mark vindicated.

ACT VI.—Two years later. Uncle Bob enters society. Charlie Hilton's unexpected return. Constancy rewarded. Cherry inherits a fortune. Billy Oliver learns golf, and wins out by a big margin. Final union of "LABOR AND CAPITAL."

Cherry, or Labor vs. Capital.

———o———

ACT ONE.

SCENE.—Dining room of humble home. Furniture, couch, three chairs, small side-table upon which are placed wash-bowl, pitcher, soap and towel. Table laid for tea. Present, Jennie Goodwin, middle aged woman. Costume, house dress becoming the wife of a mechanic.

Jennie standing by the tea table placed in center, arranging tea things :

JENNIE—"I wonder why Mark doesn't come? He said he was going to run in on his way home and look at the new Engine which has just been received by the EAGLE HOSE COMPANY, No. 7. (Laughs.) And dear me ! Just let Mark get down to the Engine House talking to the boys, and he never knows how time flies, especially if there is any new machinery to admire. Well, well; I must not scold him—even if the tea is spoiled by long waiting ; for Mark has always been a good, kind husband to me. Oh ! there he comes now."

[Enters right entrance Mark Goodwin, middle-aged man, robust, hustling, cheerful. Costume, carpenter's working suit. Crosses to tea table.]

MARK (cheerfully)—"Hello Jennie ! Kept you waiting did I, eh? Well I couldn't help it, for I tell you, Jennie, she's the prettiest thing I ever looked at.''

JENNIE, (pausing in her work of polishing glass on towel)—''Well, I like that Mark Goodwin; you certainly have your nerve with you, to stand up here before your own wife and talk about another woman's beauty.''

[Turns away with offended dignity, and walks to opposite side of the table. Mark follows, and both pause.]

MARK (in conciliatory tone)—''Come, come now, Jennie, don't go to getting on your ear. Why, my dear, there is no woman in the world half as handsome, in my eyes, as you are; why you're just as pretty as you were when I marrfed you twenty years ago. (Laughs.) Ha, ha. You thought I was talking about some pretty woman or another, when I was only praising the new Engine that has just arrived for the EAGLE HOSE COMPANY, No. 7. It wouldn't take much to make you right down jealous, would it now, Jennie?''

[Jennie mollified, and busying herself again with the table.]

JENNIE—''Oh, it was the new Engine you were talking about, eh? Well, why didn't you say so at first and not give my nerves such a shock? So it is really pretty, is it?''

MARK (enthusiastically)—''Just as pretty as a picture. Trim and neat as a lady; with all its ma-

chinery shining and flashing like gold. Oh! the
EAGLE HOSE COMPANY may well be proud of this
new beauty, my dear."

JENNIE—"I'll go down with you to-morrow evening and see it. But come, let's have supper. I'm
afraid that the tea is already spoiled by long standing."

MARK—"All right, little woman, but just let me
wash up a bit first."

[Crosses to side table pours water from pitcher
to bowl, takes soap, washes his hands and face,
takes towel, wipes face, and as he is wiping hands,
walks back to tea table. Jennie busy with tea
things.]

MARK—"Jennie, where is Cherry, hasn't she come
home yet?" (Throws towel on chair back.)

JENNIE—"No, she hasn't come yet, but we won't
wait on her. It's time she was here surely."

MARK—"Well, I should say so."

[Both seat themselves at tea table. Mark helps
plates. Jennie pours out tea.]

MARK—"Jennie, I don't like the idea of Cherry
being out on the street as much as she has been
lately. She is growing very handsome, and she's
getting to be a bit vain too. Don't you think so?"

JENNIE (pouring Mark a cup of tea)—"Yes,
Mark, Cherry is handsome. Just as handsome as
she can be. But I don't think she's vain. What
makes you think so?"

MARK (stirring cup of tea vigorously with tea-spoon)—"Well it seems to me that Cherry shows an inclination of late to snub working people, those of her own class you know; and I don't like it, Jennie I don't like it one bit. It looks as if the girl was putting on airs that don't become her."

JENNIE (spreading bread with butter)—"Well, you see Mark, the rich people have made so much of our girl; and she really is as much of a lady as if she were the daughter of a millionaire. Why, just think of it, the Deans invited her to tea last week and young Mr. Rudolph Dean walked home with her in the evening, and he never was known before to walk with a girl who didn't belong to his own set. Why, Mark, you ought to be proud of your daughter. She is so clever and accomplished, and this is why the wealthy Deans have taken such a liking to her."

MARK (eating bread and butter)—"Well, I don't like it. It won't do the girl any good; only put foolish notions into her head, and get her into no end of trouble. (Listens.) I believe I hear her coming now."

[Enters left entrance Cherry and Rudolph Dean. Cherry a charming young lady. Costume white, arranged with tasteful simplicity. Hat and gloves. Rudolph Dean a wealthy young man, dressed with exquisite taste and in the height of fashion—walking costume, cane, hat, etc., in hand. Rudolph Dean and Cherry smiling, much pleased with each other's company. Mark and Jennie rise from table, advance to the center. Meet Rudolph Dean and Cherry.]

CHERRY—"I was belated, papa, and Mr. Dean kindly brought me home."

MARK (sulkily)—"Good evening, Mr. Dean."

RUDOLPH DEAN—"Good evening, Mark. Good evening, Mrs. Goodwin."

JENNIE—"Good evening, Mr. Dean. It was very kind of you, sir, to see Cherry safe home. Won't you have a cup of tea?"

RUDOLPH DEAN—"Thank you, Mrs. Goodwin, I should like to, but I really must not stay. (Turns to Mark.) I am pleased to see you looking so well, Mark. That new block you are erecting is going to be an ornament to the city. Don't you think so?"

MARK (still sulkily)—"Oh! it will pass I guess."

RUDOLPH DEAN—"Well, good evening, Mrs. Goodwin. Miss Cherry, I am delighted that I have had the pleasure of serving you. Good evening."

JENNIE and CHERRY—"Good evening, Mr. Dean." (R. D. bows, exits.)

[Cherry begins to pull off her gloves in a confused manner, Jennie returns to table.]

MARK (half angrily)—"Cherry, what business have you to be galavanting around with young Dean? This is twice now that he has walked home with you this week."

JENNIE (from the other side of the table)—"Now Mark, don't scold Cherry. What harm has the child done by allowing Mr. Dean to walk home with her, I should like to know?"

MARK—"Well, I don't approve of Mr. Dean's attentions to her, as I have told you before; and now I positively forbid her to have anything whatever to do with him."

CHERRY (in a tremulous tone)— 'You are very hard on me, papa. Mr. Dean is a gentleman, I am sure."

MARK—"That's all right, Cherry. Mr. Dean may be, as you say, a gentleman. If he is he will prove it by choosing his associates from the monied aristocracy, and not by trying to put foolish notions into the head of a poor carpenter's daughter."

[Cherry is much hurt, and presses her handkerchief to her eyes. Jennie crosses over, stands by Cherry's side, and looks at Mark angrily.]

JENNIE—"Now you've made the poor child cry, and I hope you are satisfied, Mark Goodwin."

[Mark steps close to Cherry, puts his arms around her and draws her head to his shoulder.]

MARK (in a softened voice)—"There, there, Cherry; don't cry. Papa doesn't want to be hard on you, pet. But don't let your heart go wandering after false gods, my girl. Stick to your own friends. They are honest and loyal; but they don't belong to the class to which Mr. Dean belongs.

Let me tell you, my child, when a young man of Mr. Dean's position shows particular attentions to a young woman of your position, he doesn't mean any good by it. So be warned by your father, who knows so much more about the wicked ways of this world than you do, and stick to your own class and don't be deceived by our enemies—the rich. There, dry your tears now, and let your mother give you some tea."

[Kisses and releases her. Jennie takes Cherry's arm and leads her to a chair at the table. Cherry sits down.]

MARK—"Jennie, I am going down town, and as the EAGLE HOSE COMPANY has a meeting to-night I shall not be home before 10 or 11 o'clock."

JENNIE—"All right, Mark."

[Exit Mark left entrance. Jennie prepares cup and saucer, and takes up tea pot to pour tea.]

CHERRY—"Don't pour tea for me, mother, please. I don't want any." (Jennie puts down the tea pot.)

JENNIE—"What's the matter, Cherry? Are you ill, dear?"

[Jennie moves to the side of the table, sits down in a chair beside Cherry, and takes the girl's hand.]

CHERRY—"No, mother, I am not ill, but father has hurt my feelings very much. He is very hard on me."

JENNIE—"Your father doesn't mean to be hard

on you, darling ; but he has no faith in rich people where the welfare of the poor is concerned. This is the reason he distrusts and objects to Mr. Dean, my child, and not because he wants to be hard on you."

CHERRY—"Mr. Dean is a gentleman, mother—a noble gentleman, and incapable of wronging any woman."

JENNIE—"This may be so, my child, and I sincerely hope it is. But Cherry, my darling little daughter, your father has requested you not to receive further attentions from Mr. Dean, and I know that you will obey him. (Cherry looks straight before her and answers not a word—short pause.) Why, Cherry, just think of Charlie Hilton! It would break the poor boy's heart if he thought you cared for the attentions of Mr. Dean. Charlie is such a noble young man ; a natural born gentleman, a good mechanic, sober and industrious, and one of the most faithful members of the EAGLE HOSE COMPANY. He loves you, Cherry, and I thought you loved him."

[Cherry snatches her hand away from her mother and springs to her feet, and begins to pile up the dishes.]

CHERRY—"Let us not talk any more on the subject, mother. I will help you clear the table and then I wish to retire to my own room." (Jennie stands.)

JENNIE—"Oh, you needn't help me with the table, Cherry. You are not well ; go to your room, my dear."

CHERRY—"Good-night, mother."

JENNIE (kisses her)—"Good-night, Cherry. God bless you, dear."

[Exit Cherry. Jennie (stage business) turns back to the table, deftly removes dishes to sideboard. Takes off and folds table cloth ; puts it on sideboard. Takes dark cloth which lies on sideboard, unfolds and spreads it on table. Talks while she works.]

JENNIE—"It is too bad, too bad. I declare it is too bad. I wish Cherry had never met Mr. Dean. Before she knew him she was happy and contented, chatted, smiled and sang all the day long, and now I fear very much that there is trouble ahead for all of us. (Some one knocks at the door.) Come in !"

[Enter Charlie Hilton, dressed in a fireman's uniform, cap in hand. Jennie crosses to center.]

JENNIE—"Why, good evening, Charlie. I thought you were down at the EAGLE HOSE COMPANY's club meeting ! Mark went some time ago. Sit down, won't you ?"

[Stage business. Charlie seems to be very gloomy. They seat themselves on sofa.]

JENNIE—"So you didn't go to the club meeting, Charlie ?"

CHARLIE (very despondently) — "Yes, Mrs. Goodwin, I went to the meeting, but I felt so badly that the President excused me."

JENNIE—"You felt badly? Are you ill, Charlie?"

CHARLIE—"No, Mrs. Goodwin, but I am deeply troubled about something."

JENNIE—"Troubled about something, Charlie? (Laughs softly.) The idea of a healthy young man of good manners and sound morals being troubled about anything. Tell me about it, Charlie. I'll wager that it is all imaginary."

CHARLIE—"You wouldn't laugh if you were a young man, as I am, and in love with some one who didn't return your affections, Mrs. Goodwin."

JENNIE (elevating her hands in surprise(—"Juust hear the foolish boy talk! Now who in the world are you in love with who doesn't return your affections?"

CHARLIE—"Mrs. Goodwin, is it Cherry. Your charming, but cruel-hearted daughter, Cherry.

JENNIE—"Oh, you wrong her, Charlie. I am sure that Cherry cares for you."

CHARLIE—"I flattered myself at one time that this was true, but of late she scarcely notices me, and doesn't seem to care for any one except that soft-handed young dandy, Rudolph Dean. (Clenches right hand furiously.) Curse him!"

JENNIE—"Hush-sh-sh, Charlie! Are you not ashamed of yourself, to be so wicked!"

CHARLIE (springing to his feet)—"Wicked! If anything would put murder in a man's heart this would. To have this young coxcomb, just because he is wealthy, to be permitted to thrust himself between me and my life's happiness."

[Turns quickly away, clenches his hands together, walks to center. Jennie follows him.]

JENNIE—"Charlie, listen to me, boy. To-night Cherry's father forbade her receiving any further attentions from Mr. Dean."

CHARLIE (lifts his head and says eagerly)—"Did she promise to obey him, Mrs. Goodwin?"

JENNIE—"Well—she didn't exactly promise anything. But Cherry is a good girl, Charlie. She will never go against her father's wishes."

CHARLIE (grows despondent again)—"Money is a powerful factor in winning a woman's heart, Mrs. Goodwin."

JENNIE—"For shame, Charlie. To insinuate that our Cherry would be guilty of such weakness. You are unreasonably jealous, my boy; and let me warn you. Jealousy is a monster who opens the gate of suspicion and pushes love broken-hearted from the garden of happiness."

[Charlie goes up to the table and picks up his cap; Jennie follows him.]

JENNIE—"What! Are you going so soon, Charlie? If you will wait a moment I'll call Cherry, and she will soon put matters right between you."

CHARLIE—"Thank you, Mrs. Goodwin. But I think it is best for me not to see Miss Cherry to-night. I may be, as you say, unreasonably jealous and might be tempted to say something to the woman I love which would be unworthy of my manhood."

[Starts toward the left entrance, Jennie following him.]

JENNIE—"Oh, Charlie; I forgot to tell you. Flossie is coming to-morrow."

CHARLIE (turning back)—"I beg your pardon, Mrs. Goodwin, but who is Flossie?"

JENNIE—"Why, hasn't Cherry told you about her cousin Flossie? She is the daughter of my brother, Robert Maxwell. The child was born and reared in the wilds of New Mexico. '' mother died when she was a baby, but my br h 's always kept this, his only child, with i e is now 16 years of age, and her father h has grown quite wealthy, is bringing her home to be educated. She will be so much company for Cherry. You must come and get acquainted with my niece. You will, won't you Charlie?"

CHARLIE—"I shall be delighted to do so, Mrs. Goodwin, if you think Miss Cherry will not snub me."

JENNIE (laughs)—"Snub you! Of course she will not, you foolish boy."

CHARLIE—"Well, then, expect me. Good-night, Mrs. Goodwin."

JENNIE—"Good-night, Charlie!"

[Turns, walks back to table, smoothes the cloth down with her hands and puts chairs and things to rights. Talks to herself.]

JENNIE (laughs)—"There is nothing in this wide world that makes me half so weary as a love-sick boy. If I had one in the house with me all the time I should make old Dr. Hood rich by taking so much of his sarsaparilla for 'that tired feeling.' (Laughs.) Well, I don't believe there is any use for me to wait for Mark—there is no telling how late the fire laddies may remain at their club rooms to-night." (Takes small lamp from table, and exit left entrance.)

[Enters Cherry right entrance, with small lighted lamp (stage business) in hand, wick turned low. Walks stealthily. Places lamp on table, presses hand on heart, listens eagerly, speaks.]

CHERRY—"I ought not to see him; but I must, just this one time more, to tell him that our sweet love-dream is over. (A knock at the door.) Come in!" (softly.)

[Enters Rudolph Dean. Cherry meets him in center. He takes both her hands in his.]

RUDOLPH DEAN (with great tenderness)—"My darling!"

[Folds her in his arms and kisses her. Cherry gently releases herself.]

CHERRY—"Oh, Rudolph. I have bad news to tell you, dear."

RUDOLPH DEAN—"Why, my darling! How serious you look! What is it, little one?"

CHERRY (voice tremulous)—"My father has forbidden me to see you again."

RUDOLPH DEAN—"Forbidden you to see me again! Why has he done this cruel thing, Cherry?"

CHERRY—"Simply because you are a wealthy man, and my father says that as such your attentions to a poor carpenter's daughter cannot be honorable."

RUDOLPH DEAN—"Cherry, you know that your father misjudges me, do you not, little one?"

CHERRY—"Certainly. But how am I to make him understand his mistake?"

RUDOLPH DEAN—"By being loyal to me, your own true love, my darling."

[Cherry lifts her head suddenly in alarm; turns face towards the door, and listens.]

CHERRY (terrified)—"Oh, Rudolph! My father is coming! Go, go! For the love of heaven, go quickly!"

RUDOLPH DEAN—"Cherry, be true to me, darling!" (Hurried kiss.)

[Quick exit Rudolph Dean right entrance, and Cherry turns around and meets father, entering, left entrance.]

MARK GOODWIN—"Hello, Bobolink, haven't you retired yet?"

CHERRY (timidly)—"No, papa."

MARK (looks at her suspiciously)—"Come and sit beside me, Cherry. I want to talk to you."

CHERRY (aside in an alarmed voice)—"Oh, merciful heavens! I wonder if he saw Rudolph leaving the house?" (Goes sits beside father on sofa.)

CHERRY—"What is it, papa?"

MARK—"I saw Charlie Hilton down at the club this evening, and the boy feels awfully cut up about something. What have you done to him, Cherry?"

CHERRY (looks down at her hands confusedly)—"Nothing, papa." (Mark regards her a moment in silence.)

MARK—"Cherry, why did you decline to let Charlie Hilton walk home with you this evening, and afterwards permit young Dean to accompany you?"

CHERRY (lifts her head with a show of spirit)—"Because I wished to do so, papa."

MARK (sternly)—"Cherry, I have spoken to you about the preference you have shown for Rudolph Dean's company before, and now I warn you, girl, that if I ever hear of you speaking to this young Jackanapes again I intend to kill him. No rich man shall come fooling around my one ewe lamb, just to break her heart and ruin her life! Those wealthy devils think that we poor, laboring people have no protection against them, and that they may with impunity enter the hallowed precincts of our humble homes, and leave destruction and ruin behind them. Let them beware! They will find that even the worm will turn when it is trodden upon.''

CHERRY—''Your words do Mr. Dean an awful injustice, papa. You do not know him or you would know that he is a gentleman, and incapable of ignoble conduct.''

MARK—''That's all right, Cherry, but if Rudolph Dean knows when he is well off, he will keep out of your way and mine too. (Draws a telegram from his vest pocket.) Where's your mother? I have a telegram from your uncle Bob, which says that he and Flossie will arrive to-night. Listen! I hear voices in the hall. I shouldn't be surprised if they have already arrived.''

[Enters right entrance Jennie, Uncle Bob, and Flossie. Uncle Bob attired in regular cow boy costume. Flossie in girlish dress reaching half way between knees and ankles, black sateen underclothing. Uncle Bob holds somberno in his hands. Flossie very bright and jigantic, characteristic, petted and indulged child. Mark and Cherry, rise.]

MARK (with outstretched hand to Uncle Bob — ''Hello, old man, so it really is you, is it?'' (Shakes hands.)

UNCLE BOB—''Yas, what thare is left of me. But dog my sheep, if I wouldn't ruther go on a month's round-up than to take another sich a long journey in the cars. I'm plum beat out."

[Cherry and Flossie embrace and converse inaudibly, while Uncle Bob speaks. Uncle Bob turns to Cherry.]

UNCLE BOB—"Why, bless my soul! Is this Cherry? She has got to be sich a fine young lady Uncle Bob's most afeered to kiss her." (Takes her hands.)

CHERRY (laughs)—"Oh, you needn't be afraid, Uncle Bob."

UNCLE BOB—"Sensible to the last." (Kisses her.)

[Flossie runs and throws her arms around Mark's neck and kisses him.]

FLOSSIE—"I am so glad to see you, dear old Uncle Mark. (Takes her arms from around his neck and looks at him archly.) What do you think? Dad is going to let me stay with you two or three years, so that you may teach me to be a fine young lady like my cousin Cherry. Won't that be fine!"

MARK—"Why, you are a fine young lady now, Flossie."

FLOSSIE (laughs)—"Oh, no, Uncle Mark. I am nothing but a horrid little Mexican, and don't know anything except how to shoot a rifle, ride a bronco and dance a jig."

[Uncle Bob, Jennie and Cherry, who have been

engaged in an inaudible conversation in the background, join Mark and Flossie in the center.)

UNCLE BOB (proudly)—"Mark, what do you think of my little gal? Ain't she a cute little trick?"

MARK—"She is, for a fact!"

UNCLE BOB (very proudly)—"Why, she's gone with me on the fall round-ups every year now for three years, and dog my sheep, if she ain't worth a half dozen cow boys. But that's all over now, and sister Jennie here, and Cherry, and all the teachers they can git, has got to larn her music, grammer, 'rithmatic, history and gography; 'sides larning her to simper an' bow, kertsy an' dance; and smile when she's mad, and look sorry when she's glad, jist like all the society wemin do."

FLOSSIE—"Oh, daddy, dear. I alre .ly ' now how to dance."

UNCLE BOB—"That's a fact, Flossie. ʰh ʸ ɔan't larn you nothing about dancing, 'cepting it be new figures. You know all 'bout the steps, shoah."

CHERRY—"Who taught her to dance, Uncle Bob?"

UNCLE BOB—"Nobody. Hit jist come natchurel to her same as the birds larn to sing."

[Flossie laughs and takes a few dancing steps.]

UNCLE BOB—"Jist look at her! She can hardly keep her little feet still. Stand back a little. Thare, that's right, baby lam', show the folks how you can dance."

[All stand aside, leaving the stage free for the dancer. Orchestra plays a Mexican dance. Flossie dances to perfection for a few minutes, when the music changes to a lively cotillion, in which all the figures on the stage join.]

UNCLE BOB—"All hands 'round." (All circle around.)

QUICK CURTAIN.

FOOT NOTE.--When presented by Amateurs a song may be substituted for Flossie's dance if desired. The text then, of course, will have to be changed accordingly, substituting the words sing and song for dance. Let the song be catchy, up-to-date composition, with chorus in which the whole company joins. Curtain when singing the last stanza.—AUTHOR.

ACT TWO.

TWO MONTHS LATER.—FOREST SCENE.—A RUSTIC
BENCH.

Enters right entrance Cherry in walking costume,
hat, parasol, etc. Presses hand on heart and listens eagerly. Stands in center :

CHERRY—"Oh, the cruelty of my father that
drives me to those clandestine meetings ! Every
fibre of my being revolts at the deception I am
forced to practice. But I cannot—I will not—give
up my love. (Enters left entrance Rudolph Dean,
who walks to center, takes off hat, folds Cherry in
his arms and kisses her. Cherry releases herself
gently.) Oh, Rudolph, I was growing so terribly
nervous I was on the point of running away and
not waiting for you, dear."

RUDOLPH DEAN (fondly)—"What made you
nervous, little one ?"

CHERRY—"Rudolph, what if my father should
discover our clandestine meetings?"

[Both walk and sit on rustic bench towards stage
front.]

RUDOLPH DEAN (very fondly, smiling)—"Then
my precious one, I should tell him that I love you,
and intend to make you my wife, with or without
his consent."

CHERRY (despondently)—"My father will never

give his consent to our union, never! Mother and
I have tried all our persuasive powers upon him,
but to no purpose."

RUDOLPH DEAN—"Why does he so despise me,
Cherry?"

CHERRY—"I know no reason, except that his
deep-rooted prejudice against the wealthy class
really amounts to a monomania with my poor
father. He imagines that rich people are sworn
enemies of the poor or laboring classes, and that
nothing gives them more pleasure than to witness
the destitution, and even degredation, of the working people."

RUDOLPH DEAN—"Why, this is the spirit of so-
cialism, my love!"

CHERRY—"I don't know what it is. I only
know, to my sorrow, that my father despises and
distrusts all wealthy and aristocratic people."

RUDOLPH DEAN—"But after all, my little one,
we should have no aristocracy in our land, the free-
dom of which was purchased with the blood of our
forefathers—except that built by the true nobility
of man's character, be he rich or poor. If my
wealth, which came to me as most fortunes come
to their possessors in our country, by the mere ac-
cident of my father's business foresight, is to debar
me from the blessing of claiming the only woman
I love, or ever will love, as my wife, then it is
nothing but a curse to me."

[Enters Flossie and Billy Oliver. Flossie carries her sun-bonnet in her hand and has a small basket on her arm. Billy Oliver in bicycle suit, fishing tackle on his shoulder.]

FLOSSIE (hurriedly as the two cross over to Cherry and Mr. Dean)—"Oh, Cherry, come and see what a long string of fish we caught, and we saw an alligator and two wild cats"—

[Stops suddenly and stares at Mr. Dean. Cherry and Mr. Dean rise to their feet.]

CHERRY—"Flossie, dear, permit me to introduce you to Mr. Dean."

FLOSSIE (quickly, with commanding gesture of right hand)—"I beg your pardon. I don't want to know Mr. Dean, (reproachfully) and never mind, Miss Cherry, I am going to tell on you, too. Did not Uncle Mark forbid you to speak to Mr. Dean? Say now, didn't he?"

CHERRY (apologetically)—"But you see, Flossie dear——

FLOSSIE (interrupting her)—"No, there is no 'you see' about it. Uncle Mark told you not to speak to Mr. Dean, and you had no business to do it, and I am going to tell on you."

BILLY OLIVER (stepping quickly to Flossie's side)—"Come, come now, Flossie. Don't be hard on Miss Cherry. Suppose your father was to forbid you to speak to me?"

FLOSSIE (tossing her head and elevating her

chin)—"Then I shouldn't speak to you, Mr. Oliver."

BILLY (sidling close to Flossie, coaxingly)—"Oh, yes you would, Flossie; your own Billy, you know."

FLOSSIE (contemptuously mimicing his words)— "'Your own Billy, you know!' My own daddy is more to me than all the Billies in the world, and you may wager your last dollar that what he tells me to do, goes."

BILLY—"Into one ear and out at the other, eh, Flossie!"

FLOSSIE (contemptuously)—"Mr. Oliver, you're beneath my notice. Come on, Cherry, let's go back to the pic-nic grounds."

RUDOLPH DEAN—"I beg your pardon, Miss Flossie; I am sure you were only joking. You do not intend to get your cousin into trouble, do you?"

FLOSSIE (with much spirit)—"It is yourself, not I, who is trying to make trouble for my cousin. Why don't you keep away from her and let her alone, when you know that her father will not let you marry her, and she knows that she is already engaged to marry Mr. Charlie Hilton."

CHERRY (quickly)—"Oh, no, no, Flossie, you're mistaken. I am not engaged to Charlie Hilton."

FLOSSIE—"You were until Mr. Dean influenced you to disobey your father and break poor Charlie's heart. I am ashamed of you, Cherry Goodwin."

[Billy, who, while Flossie is speaking, has walked to left entrance and looked out, returns with quick steps to center group.]

BILLY—"Oh, I say ; they are coming !"

CHERRY—"Go Rudolph ! For the love of heaven don't let my father see you here." (Urges his flight with frantic gestures.)

RUDOLPH DEAN (entreatingly)—"Miss Flossie, for the love of God don't tell on your cousin."

BILLY—"She won't tell. Flossie is a good little angel."

FLOSSIE—"Oh, yes ; all but the wings. But take care ; don't put too much confidence in his goodness, or you may be badly fooled."

CHERRY—"Oh, Rudolph, go, go ! I hear them coming."

RUDOLPH DEAN (kisses Cherry hurriedly and looks at Flossie)—"Don't tell—don't tell on us, Miss Flossie. Oh, please don't tell."

FLOSSIE (elevating her hands)—"Well, of all the impertinent rascals out of jail, Mr. Dean takes the cake." (Hurried exit Mr. Dean left entrance.)

[Enter pic-nicers—Jennie, Mark, Charlie Hilton and Uncle Bob.]

UNCLE BOB—"Hello, baby lam'! Whut you all doin' up hare so long ? We blow'd the dinner horn fur you three times."

FLOSSIE—"We've been fishing, daddy dear."

[Cherry goes to rustic seat and sits down pale and dejected.]

MARK—"What's the matter, Cherry? You look as limp as a rag."

FLOSSIE (running up to Mark, who has crossed to Cherry)—"Oh, uncle Mark! (Cherry hangs her head.) What do you think? (Billy runs over to Flossie's side, pulls her dress skirt and says in a faint whisper: 'Flossie, Flossie; hush-sh-sh-sh.') We caught ten fishes, and we saw an alligator and two wild cats!" (Billy and Cherry look relieved.)

MARK—"You did, eh! Maybe the wild cats frightened Cherry. She was always afraid of wild varmints."

UNCLE BOB—"Ha, ha, ha. Afeerd of wild varmints! What do you think of that, baby lam'?"

FLOSSIE (laughs)—"We'll take her home with us and out on a few round-ups. That will take the kinks out of her. Won't it, dad?"

UNCLE BOB—"Hit shoah will, baby lam'."

JENNIE—"Come on and let's go to dinner before the coffee gets cold and the ants get all over everything."

MARK (to Cherry)—"Come on, bobolink."

CHERRY—"I don't want any dinner, papa; my head aches. I'll come when I feel better."

UNCLE BOB—"Mark, Cherry seems to be mighty funny, somehow. I guess Flossie and me had better go back to Mexico and take Cherry with us, and let her rough it awhile."

JENNIE (Jennie sits down beside Cherry and takes her hand)—"What's the matter dear?"

CHERRY—"Nothing ; only my head aches, and I want to sit here awhile."

JENNIE—"Shall I stay with you?"

CHERRY—"No, thank you, mother. I would rather be alone."

JENNIE (rising)—"Well, come to the pic-nic grounds when you get rested. (Addressing the others.) Come on ; we must go to dinner."

CHARLIE HILTON (pausing before Cherry)— "May I bring you a cup of coffee, Miss Cherry?"

CHERRY—"No, I thank you, Mr. Hilton,"

[Exit Mark, Jennie, Uncle Bob, Flossie, Charlie Hilton and Billy Oliver. Cherry rests elbow of right arm on arm of rustic bench, and rests head on right hand. Sits motionless. Enters Rudolph Dean left entrance, who crosses softly to Cherry's side.]

RUDOLPH DEAN— "My darling !" (Cherry starts up in alarm.)

CHERRY—"Rudolph ! Oh, my love ! Why did you come again? We may be discovered."

RUDOLPH DEAN (folding her in his arms)—"Fear not, little one. I reconnoitered the situation. They are all busily engaged with dinner. There is no danger. I wanted to find out if Flossie betrayed us."

[Cherry frees herself gently from his embrace.]

CHERRY—"She did not, Rudolph, although I am

nearly frightened to death for fear she will. Rudolph, I cannot practice this deception much longer. I am positively ashamed to look either of my parents in the face."

RUDOLPH DEAN—"Then, darling, if there is no hope of winning your father's consent to our marriage, there is only one way left open to us, and that is to elope."

CHERRY—"Oh, Rudolph! What a terrible alternative."

RUDOLPH DEAN (very fondly)—"No, darling, not so terrible to give your sweet self to me, your devoted lover and willing slave. Say that you will go with me, Cherry."

CHERRY (softly)—"I will think about it, Rudolph."

RUDOLPH DEAN—"And in the meantime your father may discover our clandestine meetings, and prevent our ever meeting again. Let us become man and wife this very week. You are all the world to me, sweetheart."

CHERRY—"And you are all the world to me, Rudolph."

RUDOLPH DEAN—"Then, my darling, meet me to-morrow night at our old trysting place in your father's orchard, and we will soon be beyond all cruel intervention."

CHERRY (clasping her hands in deep emotion)— "Oh, if my father would only give his consent to our union!"

RUDOLPH DEAN—"He never will, my darling. You only consent to my plans and all will be well."

[Cherry turns her head in a startled manner and listens.]

CHERRY (alarm in her voice)—"Oh, Rudolph! I think I hear some one coming. For pity's sake, leave me before we are discovered!"

RUDOLPH DEAN (taking her hands)—"Say that you will fly with me to-morrow night, my love!"

CHERRY (in great excitement)—"Yes. Oh, go! Go quickly! Don't you hear footsteps approaching!"

[Rudolph Dean hurriedly kisses Cherry, and looks over his shoulder as he makes his exit.]

RUDOLPH DEAN—"Remember, love, to-morrow night in your father's orchard."

[Exit left entrance. Cherry sits down on the bench. Enters Charlie Hilton, who carries a cup and saucer on small tray. (Stage business.) He crosses over and stands before Cherry.]

CHARLIE—"Miss Cherry, I have brought you a cup of coffee. Your mother says that if you will drink it, it may relieve your head ache."

[Cherry takes the proffered tray and Charlie sits down beside her.]

CHERRY—"You are very kind, indeed, Charlie."
CHARLIE—"Yes, kind to myself; for nothing

gives me half as much pleasure as serving you, Miss Cherry."

[Cherry sips coffee with teaspoon.]

CHERRY—"I am not worthy of such devotion, Charlie."

CHARLIE—"Indeed you are, Miss Cherry, and I wish you would give me the right to love and serve you all my life."

CHERRY—"You will find some one better suited to be your wife than myself, Charlie."

CHARLIE—"Never! Never! There is only one woman in the world for me, and if the blessing of her love is denied me, I want no other."

[Cherry silently continues to sip the coffee, and Charlie regards her face a moment in silence.]

CHARLIE—"Miss Cherry—forgive me. I am going to ask you a question, which you may think I have no right to ask. If so, let my great love for you plead my pardon. Are you in love with Rudolph Dean?"

CHERRY (lifts her head and says earnestly)—"I am in love with Rudolph Dean. I love him more than I love any one on earth, and a thousand times more than I love life itself."

CHARLIE (in a voice of consternation)—"Miss Cherry, for the love of God be careful!"

CHERRY—"What do you mean? I do not understand you."

CHARLIE (with great earnestness)—"Rudolph Dean may be only trifling with you, and has won your love only to break your heart, and blight your life. If this be true (springs to his feet and clenches his right hand) let him beware! for as sure as the sun is now shining above us, his vile heart's blood shall pay the forfeit for his crime!"

[Enters Mark Goodwin right entrance. Charlie crosses over to left wing and stands with his back partly turned towards Mark and Cherry. Stage business.]

MARK—"Hello, bobolink! How is the head ache?"

CHERRY—"It is better, papa."

MARK—"That's good." (To Charlie.) Charlie, come here, my boy."

[Charlie turns, walks back and stands before Mark, and salutes.]

CHARLIE—"Aye, aye; Captain."

[Mark takes tray, with cup and saucer, from Cherry's lap, hands it to Charlie.]

MARK—"Take the tray back to the pic-nic grounds and tell Jennie that Cherry and myself will be there presently."

[Charlie takes the tray and touches his cap.]

CHARLIE—"All right, Captain."

[Exit right entrance. Mark sits down by the side of Cherry.]

MARK—"Well, bobolink ; you and Charlie have been making up your little quarrels, eh? That's right, my girl. Charlie is one of the most noble boys in the EAGLE HOSE COMPANY. Any girl might feel proud to win him for a husband."

[Cherry hesitates, looks down a moment at her hands clasped nervously in her lap, then lifts her head and looks into her father's face.]

CHERRY—"Papa, Charlie Hilton can never be anything more to me than he is at present. I appreciate his worth, and am proud of him as my friend, but this is as far as my feelings go toward him."

MARK (with bluff tenderness)—"Oh, come, come now, Cherry. None of that. It sounds like the silly gobble of a heroine in a dime novel."

CHERRY (earnestly)—"Nevertheless, papa, it is true. Charlie Hilton is all now that he will ever be to me."

MARK (with a voice of rising anger)—"Cherry, what in the thunder has come over you lately? I believe in my heart that you still have a hankering after that lily-fingered young Dean. Damn his pusilanimous soul !"

CHERRY (springs to her feet)—"Father, I command you to stop ! I am your daughter, sir, and a lady, and I will not permit such language in my presence !"

[Mark stands up.]

MARK (in a molified voice)—"But Cherry, it makes me so cursed—oh, I beg your pardon—so infernally mad, when I think of that rich man who has everything that wealth can purchase, who has come sneaking around trying to ruin the sunlight of my humble home, the small comforts of which were bought by the sweat of my brow, that it puts murder in my heart. Don't I see the change in you since his coming! Are you the same blithesome girl, who before you became acquainted with this man, made music and sunshine for your father's lowly cottage?"

[Cherry puts her arms around Mark's neck, and kisses him, looking him lovingly in the face.]

CHERRY—"Papa, darling! Why are you so prejudiced against Mr. Dean? He loves me, and I love him, and he wishes me to become his wife."

[Mark unwinds her arms from about his neck, holds her hands and looks sternly down into her upturned face.]

MARK (with great earnestness)—"Cherry, listen to me, little one—your own father, who would give his heart's blood for your happiness. It is not love that brings this scion of a wealthy and aristocratic house to the poor carpenter's cottage, but the meanest and most contemptible selfishness. His wealth has made it possible for him to achieve every object desired in his life. When he found out that for once he was likely to be baffled, he changes his tactics and asks your hand of me in marriage, thinking that I would be overwhelmed by the honor he had done me, supposing I had not seen through his vile scheming, and would give in marriage to this worldly and selfish man my only child, and the one blessing which alone makes the hard work a day-life of her parents endurable. How long, think you, would it have been till this pampered son of wealth would have grown tired of the prize he had won, and we should have seen you a broken-hearted wife, deserted by the man who had won your love only to ruin and crush your life ; and scorned by his aristocratic friends. (Cherry sinks on her knees and buries her face in her hands. Mark bends partially over her.) No, girl ; I tell you no ! Dry your tears and listen to my vow. Rather than that you should become the wife of Rudolph Dean, or be in any way connected with him, (stands erect and raises his right hand to heaven) I swear before Almighty God, I WILL MURDER HIM !"

CURTAIN.

ACT THREE.

Cherry (despairingly)—"What an unfortunate creature I am! How my heart is torn between love and filial duty. Shall I disobey my father or be false to my own true love? (Draws letter from her pocker, unfolds and reads aloud) :

'Be true to your love vows, my darling, and God will bless you. Do not permit your father's threats to intimidate you. I do not fear him, my love, and when he has seen what a devoted husband I shall make, and how my mother loves and respects the sweet wife of my own choice, he will be cured of his madness, and there will be peace and happiness between us. I have all in readiness for our flight, and shall await your coming at the old trysting place to-night at 11 o'clock. My precious one, do not fail me. Your devoted RUDOLPH.'

(Clasps her hands and exclaims in agony): "God have mercy upon me! What shall I do? (Lifts her head with sudden resolution.) My beloved, I will fly with you, and bravely face the consequences."

[Hears footsteps approaching—quickly hides letter in her pocket. Enter right entrance, Jennie, Uncle Bob and Flossie, laughing in high spirits.]

Uncle Bob (breezily)—"Whut do you think, Cherry? I've jist got a note from that young tenderfoot, Billy Oliver, asken me for Flossie! For

Flossie now! My pet and baby! And all I have to love in the world! Did you ever hear of sich impudence? I'll swan. I've a notion to break his neck!"

FLOSSIE—"Oh, dad! Don't be hard on Billy. He's awful nice."

UNCLE BOB—"Hard on Billy! Thunderation. It ain't hard on your old dad to give you up? Oh, no!"

FLOSSIE—"But you'd have to give me up some day you know, daddy dear."

JENNIE—"That's so, brother Bob. The boys will coax the girls away from the old folks sooner or later. Now here's Cherry—I shouldn't be surprised any day to hear that she and Charlie Hilton had decided to make a match. (Cherry turns away abruptly, goes to the table and begins to turn the leaves of a book thereon.) But it's all right, I guess. We did the same way when we were young, you know."

UNCLE BOB—"It's pretty hard on the old folks, though Jennie, to jist git a gal up to whar she's some comfort to you, when up walks some smart young Alick, without as much as hardly sayen' 'dog, will ye bite!' and walks off with her."

FLOSSIE (brightening up)—"But you see, dear old dad, it will be different with Billy and me, for we will always live with you."

UNCLE BOB (lugubriously)—"Guess you will,

baby lam', for whut's Billy got to keep you on?
Nothen that I knows on.''

FLOSSIE—"Why, dad! He's got his typewriter,
and his bicycle !''

UNCLE BOB—"That's a fact.''

FLOSSIE—"And you're going to get me a wheel,
and get you a wheel ; then won't we three have
fun going on the round-ups on bicycles instead of
broncos !'' (Clasps her hands in delight.)

UNCLE BOB (dryly)—"Shoar.''

[Cherry crosses to group in center.]

CHERRY—"But, Uncle Bob, what about Flossie's
education? She has only been to school about two
months since she came here, and now you are talking about her marriage.''

UNCLE BOB (decisively)—"Oh, Flossie's got to
go to school two years, shoar ; and then if her Billy
shows hisself to be a man—why, then we'll talk
about this other business. Why, Flossie is nothen
but a baby yet.''

JENNIE—"Well, I should say so.''

FLOSSIE—"But I'm engaged, ain't I dad?''

UNCLE BOB—"Oh, I reckon so. But mind, the
schoolen comes fust.''

JENNIE—"There, Flossie ; I think you might
give us a jig for that.''

UNCLE BOB—"Shoar !''

FLOSSIE—"All right. Please stand out of the
way.''

[Jennie and Cherry sit on sofa. Uncle Bob in a chair. Flossie dances to music of the orchestra. (*See foot note.) When dance is finished Flossie, laughingly, (stage business) sits down on ottoman placed near the sofa.]

CHERRY—"What a suple little creature you are, Flossie dear."

UNCLE BOB (laughs)—"You'd say so, shoar, if you could see her swing the lariat onct."

FLOSSIE (laughs)—"I told you, cousin Cherry, that I'm nothing but a little savage." (All laugh.)

CHERRY (suddenly)—"Mother, where is father this evening?"

JENNIE—"He went to Winston this afternoon."

CHERRY (anxiously)—"When will he return?"

JENNIE—"To-night about midnight."

UNCLE BOB—"How did he go?"

JENNIE—"He went on horseback."

UNCLE BOB—"I wisht he'd a tole me he wus agoen, and I'd a gone with him."

JENNIE—"He went away in such a hurry that he did not say anything about going to any one but myseli."

UNCLE BOB—"Mark acts like he had somethen or 'nother on his mind that was pestering him might-ly lately."

---

*The dance here may be omitted, and a song substituted—or both may be omitted, taking the conversation from "the schoolen comes fust" to Cherry's question "mother, where's father," etc.

CHERRY (gets up)—"Mother, if you will excuse me I will retire to my room—I have some letters to write."

JENNIE (stands)—"Certainly, my dear."

CHERRY (kisses Jennie)—"Good-night, dearest and best of mothers. Will you always love your Cherry, no matter what she may do?"

JENNIE—"Certainly, darling. But you look so serious! What is the matter, child?"

CHERRY (smiling)—"Never mind; kiss father good-night for me. Good-night. (Kisses Jennie again and turns to Uncle Bob—Uncle Bob stands.) Good-night, dear Uncle Bob. (Kisses him and turns to Flossie—Flossie stands.) Good-night, sweet child, God bless you."

FLOSSIE—"Good-night, cousin Cherry. Don't forget that you have promised to take me to the park in the morning before school time. (Kisses her. Exit Cherry left entrance.) How funny cousin Cherry acted! She kissed us all and said 'good-night' as solemnly as if she were never coming back."

UNCLE BOB—"She did, fur a fact. Whut's the matter with that gal, sister? 'Pears to me that she's in love, or trouble, or something."

[Flossie crosses to table, turns leaves of photograph album placed on table.]

JENNIE (sighs)—"I don't know, brother Bob. Cherry's disposition has undergone a marvelous change within the last few months, and it seems as if she is growing away from us somehow."

Uncle Bob—"Maybe you've edicated her too much, and that it has made a case like the young eagle in the sparrer's nest, eh, Jennie!"

Jennie—"Oh, I hope not, brother Bob."

Flossie—"Daddy dear, have you seen those lovely photographs?"

Uncle Bob—"No, baby lam'."

Flossie—"Come here and I will show them to you."

[Uncle Bob and Jennie cross to table.]

Jennie—"I will show him the pictures. Go and see who is knocking at the door, Flossie dear."

[Jennie takes album and sits beside Uncle Bob on sofa. Turns leaves, converses (stage business) inaudibly. Flossie goes and opens the door. Enters Billy Oliver in bicycle costume.]

Flossie (taking both of Billy's hands)—"Oh, Billy! I have something awful good to tell you."

Billy (anxiously)—"Have you, Flossie? What is it, sweetheart?"

Flossie—"Why, we're engaged!"

Billy—"Oh, goody! goody! (Anxiously.) Did your father say so, Flossie?"

Flossie—"Yes; and he is going to buy me a bicycle, and him a bicycle, and then you'll take your bicycle, and we will all go out on the round-ups, when we go home, on bicycles instead of broncos. Won't that be fun?"

BILLY—"No end of fun ! But when are we to be married, Flossie?"

FLOSSIE—"Oh, not for two years yet."

BILLY (gaspingly)—"Not for two years yet? Why, Flossie ! You'll jilt me long before that time expires for some other fellow !"

FLOSSIE (drops his hands, puts her hands behind her and elevates her chin—saucily)—"Well, perhaps I shall, Mr. Oliver. Girls are mighty fickle, you know."

BILLY (despairingly)—"Oh, Flossie——"

UNCLE BOB (crossing quickly to Billy and Flossie)—"Hello, young folks ! Whut's the racket?"

BILLY (appealing)—"Miss Flossie says, sir, that we shall not be married for two years from this time !"

UNCLE BOB—"Hump ! And who said that Flossie would ever marry you, young man ?"

BILLY (very humbly)—"The young lady said so herself, sir."

UNCLE BOB—"She did, eh ? Well, she's nothen but a kid. You'd better git her daddy's sentiments on the subject."

BILLY—"You will give Flossie to me, won't you, sir ?"

UNCLE BOB—"Give Flossie to you ! Well, I'll swan ! Young man, you've got sand enough to plaster a house ; dog my sheep if you ain't !"

FLOSSIE (places her hand entreatingly on Uncle

Bob's arm)—"There, there, daddy dear. Please
don't be hard on the poor fellow. He loves me,
and says that he will make a splendid husband for
me."

UNCLE BOB (in a hurt tone)—"All right, baby
lam', if you're so anxious to leave your old dad.
(Turns to Billy.) But say, young feller, 'sposen
now that I should give my little gal to you, will
you be good enough to tell me whut means of support you have?"

BILLY (brightening up—speaks proudly)—"It is
universally admitted, sir, that I have the finest pair
of bicycle legs in the country."

JENNIE (running up to center group, laughing)—
"Oh, he's well equipped for life, brother Bob.
You needn't worry about that."

[Enters Charlie Hilton in great haste and excitement.]

CHARLIE HILTON—"Mrs. Goodwin, where is the
Captain?"

JENNIE—"Why, for the land's sake, Charlie Hilton, how you scared me! What's the matter?"

CHARLIE HILTON—"Where is Captain Mark?"

JENNIE—"He has gone to Winston. What do you
want with him? Is there anything the matter?"

CHARLIE HILTON (aside)—"Merciful heavens!
How can I break the news to them?"

UNCLE BOB (sternly)—"Come, speak up Charlie,
what's the matter man? Your face is as pale as a
tenderfoot's at a lychen."

CHARLIE HILTON (desperately) — "Rudolph Dean has been found murdered in Captain Goodwin's orchard, with Miss Cherry's insensible form lying not more than a dozen feet away from the murdered man's body!"

[Great consternation in the stage group. Stage business.]

JENNIE (clasping her hands to her head frantically)—"What? Oh, my God! What has happened to my child?"

FLOSSIE—"Charlie, you are playing a cruel joke on us."

UNCLE BOB (shaking his fist at Charlie)—"If you are, young man, you shall take the goldarndest thrashen that ever a tenderfoot got."

CHARLIE HILTON—"Come and see for yourselves!"

[All rush in confusion from the stage. Exit left entrance. Enters right entrance Mark Goodwin in full riding costume, whip, spurs, ect.—appearance of having ridden long and hard—looks about the room curiously.]

MARK—"Well, well. I wonder if everybody has gone to bed this early? (Takes out his watch and looks at it.) By jacks! It is later than I thought it was! No wonder that everybody is in bed, and it is high time that I was in bed, too. But I wonder why they left the lamps burning? And come to think of it, I saw a bright light burning in Cherry's room, and Dr. Michaux's horse and buggy standing before our street gate as I rode up. I hope no one is ill."

[Enters Jennie, her hair in disorder ; evidence of weeping on her face.]

JENNIE (with much emotion)—"Oh, Mark ! Mark ! I am so glad that you've returned ! What made you stay so late ?"

MARK (soothingly)—"Why, little woman, I came as soon as I could. Remember, it is a long distance from here to Winston."

JENNIE (clasping her hands with a despairing gesture)—"Oh, a dreadful thing has happened to-night."

MARK (huskily)—"What do you mean, Jennie? Is there anything the matter with Cherry ? (Jennie buries her face in her hands and sobs wildly. Mark shakes her by the shoulder, his voice greatly agitated.) Jennie, speak woman ! Tell me the worst. I am a man, and will bear my sorrow as a man should. Has the sunlight of our home departed forever ? Is Cherry——is our darling dead ?"

[Jennie takes her hands away from her face and looks up at Mark.]

JENNIE—"No, Mark. Thank God, Cherry is not dead—but oh, God, Mark ! Will you believe it— Rudolph Dean is dead !"

[Mark gives Jennie a slight push away from him and straightens up.]

MARK (angrily)—"Why are you making such a fuss over Rudolph Dean's death? You have half frightened me to death. (Strikes his whip angrily against his leg.) Do you suppose I will shed tears over the death of one of the poor people's enemies —a millionaire? If I and my whole family were lying dead from starvation would he or any one of his class, think you, ever give one pitying thought to the poor devils whom the cursed selfishness of the rich binds down to a life of slavery, only a degree less degrading than that of African bondage as it once existed? Shed tears over the death of a narrow-souled millionaire, indeed! Jennie, I am ashamed of you! Go to your room, woman, and shed tears over the unhappy fate of your own class, and thank God that one more of our enemies has been called to his account before the Judgment Bar of God!"

[Jennie stands with clasped hands and drooping head, her whole attitude that of despair. Enters from right entrance two uniformed police officers— one carries folded parchment in his hand. Jennie and Mark turn and meet them in center.]

FIRST OFFICER—"Mark Goodwin, in the name of the Commonwealth of North Carolina, I arrest you for the murder of Rudolph Dean!"

[Second officer stands a little behind the first officer, and eyes Mark closely while the arrest is being made.]

JENNIE—"Oh, Mark, Mark! What does the

man mean? Oh, merciful God! You are not going with those officers, are you? Why don't you tell them that you are innocent of the charge! Oh, oh, oh! (Wrings her hands in anguish.)

[Enters in great haste Uncle Bob and Flossie.]

FLOSSIE—"Oh, Aunt Jennie! What's the matter? What is the matter?"

UNCLE BOB— 'Whut's to pay, Mark? Whut air these officers here fur? Stop your sniflen, Jennie, and Flossie, and let Mark tell whut's the matter. I've got plenty of the 'whar-with-all' to git him out all right, no matter whut the fuss is about. (Turns to officers.) Whut the thunder air you here fur, anyhow, in this law-abiden house?"

FIRST OFFICER—"We came to arrest Mark Goodwin for the murder of Rudolph Dean. The man is our prisoner—don't any one dare to resist us."

[Uncle Bob's arms fall to his side, and he gazes in speechless astonishment at the officer.]

FIRST OFFICER (to Mark)—"Come on prisoner."

[Jennie throws herself on Mark's breast and clings to him, sobbing and lamenting.]

FLOSSIE (to officers, angrily)—"You are a pair of blockheads! (Stamps her foot.) And you will be ashamed of yourselves when you see what a mistake you have made."

UNCLE BOB—"Flossie, Flossie; be quiet child."

FLOSSIE (appealing to Uncle Bob)—"Oh, dad, dad ! You are not going to let those horrid men take poor uncle Mark to prison, are you ? Go on his bond—give the men money—do anything to save him from this disgrace !" (Throws herself into Uncle Bob's arms and sobs aloud.)

TABLEAUX FOR CURTAIN :

Jennie in Mark's arms, he bending his head fondly over hers. First officer trying to pull the woman away from her husband's arms. Second officer stands back of the group, with pistol drawn. Flossie in Uncle Bob's arms.

CURTAIN.

ACT FOUR.

TIME—EARLY IN THE NIGHT.

Scene—Engine House of Eagle Hose Company, No. 7. Present, members of the Company in full uniform. Charlie Hilton stands in center with note book and pencil in hand. Other members—some sitting down, others lounging or standing.

Charlie Hilton (with much feeling)—"Who would ever have thought, boys, at our last meeting when we were all so happy, and our Captain was the jolliest man in the crowd, that our next meeting would be enveloped in sadness on account of an awful misfortune which had fallen upon our beloved leader?"

Jim Tracy (a fireman)—"But Captain Mark will come out all right, Charlie. You know that he is falsely accused of the murder of Rudolph Dean."

Charlie Hilton—"Yes, I believe he is falsely accused, Jim; but he's got to prove his innocence."

John Williams (a fireman)—"The evidence is mighty strong against him, Charlie."

Jim Tracy—"But it is purely circumstancial evidence."

John Williams—"Yes, Jim; but many a man has been hung on purely circumstantial evidence. You see, our Captain hated Rudolph Dean with all the intensity of a man of strong prejudices, whose heart could be so warm and loyal to his friends and so bitter toward his enemies."

FRANK WELLS (a fireman)—"And it can be proven that Captain Goodwin swore that if his daughter, Miss Cherry, attempted to marry Mr. Dean he would murder him. Putting all this together, with the fact that Rudolph Dean was murdered on the night of his intended elopement with Miss Cherry, makes things looks mighty black for our Captain, although I don't believe, boys, that he committed the murder."

JIM TRACY—"Can't he prove an alibi?"

JOHN WILLIAMS—"No, that's the trouble; he can't prove where he was after he left Winston at 4 o'clock in the afternoon till he was arrested at 1 o'clock on the night of the murder."

JIM TRACY—"Yes, it looks pretty bad."

JOHN WILLIAMS—"You're right, Jimmie, it does look shady; but nobody will ever make me believe that our whole-souled Captain would commit murder under any circumstances."

CHARLIE HILTON—"Neither do I believe it, boys. But that's nothing here nor there. Our Captain is in trouble. He is, as we all know, a poor man, who has never been able to lay up anything for the proverbial rainy day, which comes sooner or later into every man's life; and into his life this day has fallen with no gentle down-pour, but in a furious and overwhelming storm. Are we, his friends and fellow-firemen, going to stand firmly by him during this storm? That's the question, boys."

FIREMEN (all in chorus)—"Aye, Charlie."

CHARLIE HILTON—"All right, boys. How much will each man subscribe now to help employ the best legal talent the State affords to defend him in his coming trial? See, I have headed the list with one hundred dollars!"

JIM TRACY—"Put my name down for one hundred, Charlie."

JOHN WILLIAMS—"And mind for one hundred, also."

DENNIS O'FLANIGAN (Irish fireman)—"And pit down the name of Dennis O'Flanigan fur seventy dollar, and be jabbers if it warnt fur Bridget and the shanty full of helpless kids you'd see the selfsame name 'o this boie down on the book, plidged for the sum of three hundred dollar to hilp our poor Cap'en out, fur he no more murder'd that rich spalpeen than Saint Patrick did!"

FRANK WELLS—"And put my name for fifty dollars."

ANOTHER FIREMAN—"Put mine down for twenty-five dollars."

ANOTHER FIREMAN—"And mine for twenty dollars," (and so on till every member has subscribed something.)

CHARLIE HILTON (who, while the others have

been speaking, has been writing rapidly in his memoranda)—"All right, boys. You are the kind of friends for a man to be proud to possess. Now, I propose that the legal services of Shaw & Scales be secured at once on the case. What say you?"

FIREMEN (all in chorus)—"Aye, aye; Shaw & Scales!"

CHARLIE HILTON—"Who will agree to attend to the matter, boys?"

DENNIS O'FLANIGAN—"It's mesilf phwat moves that Mr. Charlie Hilton be appinted a committee of won to take the matther in hand."

JIM TRACY—"I second the motion."

DENNIS O'FLANIGAN—"It has been moved and siconded that Mr. Charlie Hilton take the business of looken afther our Cap'ens definse in hand. All in favor say 'aye,' conthrary 'no!'"

FIREMEN (in quick chorus)—"Aye!"

DENNIS O'FLANIGAN (proudly)—"Mr. Charlie Hilton's 'lected!"

CHARLIE HILTON—"Thank you, comrades. I'll do my best."

DENNIS O'FLANIGAN (with much feeling)—"And Charlie, we want you to go ivery blissed day and visit our poor Cap'en in the jail beyants, and tell him that his boies belave in his innocence, and ivery mither's son of 'em will stand by him to the last."

JIM TRACY—"Yes, Charlie, tell him not to lose heart. He will come out all right."

DENNIS O'FLANIGAN —"That he will."

CHARLIE HILTON (closes his note book and replaces it in his pocket)—"All right, boys, you may trust me to attend to everything——"

CLANG ! CLANG ! CLANG !

[Quick, loud fire alarm from behind the scenes.]

DENNIS O'FLANIGAN (in consternation)—"Holy Mither ! Foir ! And our Cap'en not with us !"

JIM TRACY (quickly)—"Take command, Charlie !"

FIREMEN (in chorus)—"Charlie Hilton is our Captain !"

CHARLIE HILTON (in a voice of command)—"Man your ropes and on to the fire !"

[Snatches speaking trumpet and takes the lead. Exit Fire Company in haste, but perfect order. The scene is quickly shifted and discloses a two-story frame building enveloped in flames. Enters firemen, hose wagon, engine, spectators, etc.]

CHARLIE HILTON—"Turn on the water ! Is every one out of the building ?"

DENNIS O'FLANIGAN—"Yes, ivery mither's son, Saints be praised ?"

MAN IN THE CROWD—"No, there is a man in the basement !"

DENNIS O'FLANIGAN—"He'll have to doie there then ; fur no man could live a minit in them flames and that smoke !"

CHARLIE HILTON—"Quick! Where is the man located?"

VOICE IN THE CROWD—"In the basement!"

CHARLIE HILTON—"I'll bring him out!"

JIM TRACY (catching hold of Charlie)—"Charlie, for God's sake don't attempt it! It will be your sure death if you do!"

CHARLIE HILTON (angrily)—"Jim, take your hands off of me, or I'll knock you down. Do you suppose that I am afraid to die? It is a thousand times easier to die than to live after life has been deprived of all hope of happiness, as mine has been."

[Charlie dashes to the door, kicks it open and disappears in the burning building.]

DENNIS O'FLANIGAN (in a loud voice)—"Anither foirman's life sacrificed to dooty! God have mercy on his brave sowl. (Takes command.) Turn yer hose on the lift wing, me lads! Play her out! Stiddy, now! Courage! Courage! Hurrah! Hurrah! Ye'r gitten the foir under conthrol, hurrah!"

[Charlie staggers from the burning building, from the door at which he entered it—carries, wrapped in blankets, the insensible form of a man. Falls with his burden prostrate on the stage. Loud cheers from firemen and spectators.]

QUICK CURTAIN.

ACT FIVE.

SCENE -Parlor in Mark Goodwin's home—time, morning. A large screen divides the room. Present—Cherry, costume of deep mourning; sits beside table placed in center, right arm resting on table, head bowed resting on arm, face pale, and partly hidden. Enter left entrance Flossie, house costume, walks softly to Cherry's side; sadly contemplates Cherry's bowed silent figure a moment in silence. Turns, walks four steps to right, pauses facing audience.]

FLOSSIE—"Poor Cherry! I am so sorry for her I don't know what to do. It would have killed me if Billy had been murdered as poor Mr. Dean was; and Cherry must have loved Mr. Dean a great deal more than I love Billy, for she was going to elope and marry him against her father's wishes, and this I would never do for any man. If dad should look at me as he always does when he is in solid earnest and say, 'see hare, baby lam', you're not agoen to marry Billy Oliver, do yer understand?' (laughs) why I'd just simply put my arms around the old darling's neck and say, 'all right, dad, you are more to me than all the Billy Oliver's in the world, and I'll just live and die an old maid.' But poor Cherry! I wish I could say something to her to take her mind away from her trouble, if it was only for a few moments. (Drops eyes to floor, stands a moment in thoughtful silence; brightens up suddenly and clasps her hands.) Oh, I know what I'll do! I'll tell her about last night's fire. (Walks back to Cherry's side, places right hand softly on Cherry's bowed head—speaks gently.) Cherry!" (Cherry lifts her head and looks at Flossie, sadly.)

CHERRY—"What do you want, Flossie?"

FLOSSIE—"Did you hear about the fire last night, Cherry?"

CHERRY (listlessly)—"I heard the alarm, that was all."

FLOSSIE (eagerly)—"Come and sit by me on the sofa, and I will tell you all about it. (Seat themselves on sofa.) Oh, it was an awful big fire, Cherry, and the large frame building, the Morton House, on East Market street, near the postoffice, was burned to the ground."

CHERRY (with a slight show of interest)— "Couldn't the fire department save the house?"

FLOSSIE—"No; the old building was all ablaze before the fire alarm was sounded. But Cherry, I want to tell you what a brave thing Charlie Hilton did."

CHERRY (quickly)—"What did he do, Flossie?"

FLOSSIE (very enthusiastically)—"He rushed into the burning building when every one said that it would be certain death to do so, and carried out a poor miserable fellow named Jo Black, who was suffocated and unconscious from the smoke, and whose life, daddy says, wasn't worth a nickel. Wasn't it brave of Charlie?"

CHERRY (clasps her hands tightly in her lap—gaspingly)—"Was Charlie injured?"

FLOSSIE—"No, not much—only scorched a little. But, Cherry, what do you think the poor fellow said before he rushed into the burning house, to those who were trying to prevent him from going?"

CHERRY (lapsing into indifference)—"I'm sure I do not know, Flossie."

FLOSSIE —"He said, 'do you suppose that I am afraid to die? It is a thousand times easier to die than to live after life has been deprived of all hope of happiness, as mine has been.' (Cherry buries her face in her hands and sobs.) There now! (In great distress.) What have I done? Oh, dear, I am always saying something that I have no business to say. (Puts her arms around Cherry.) Don't cry, darling! Don't cry. I am such a little idiot. Please don't cry, Cherry." (Cherry removes her hands from her face and gets up.)

CHERRY—"Never mind, Flossie. Run away now, dear. I want to be alone."

FLOSSIE (stands)—"But Cherry, if you are alone you will do nothing but cry. Do try to look on the bright side of things."

CHERRY—"I'll do the best I can, Flossie. Now run up stairs, dear."

FLOSSIE (kisses her)—"Poor darling—you have so much to bear."

CHERRY—"Run away now ; won't you, dear'"

FLOSSIE—"And you won't cry after I'm gone?"

CHERRY—"No, Flossie."

[Exit Flossie left entrance. Cherry takes same position at table. Enters right entrance Mrs. Dean, middle-aged lady in deep mourning, bonnet, long veil, etc., mother of Rudolph Dean. Approaches Cherry's side and places her hand on the girl's bowed head.]

MRS. DEAN (pityingly and tenderly) — "My child!" (Cherry starts suddenly to her feet.)

CHERRY (voice full of agony)—"Oh, Mrs. Dean ! Have you come to reproach me in my grief?"

MRS. DEAN (takes Cherry's hands—voice tender)—"No, Cherry ; not to reproach, but to try to comfort you, my child."

CHERRY (in amazement)—"To comfort me ? I who have caused you so much sorrow?"

MRS. DEAN (with much feeling)—"My boy loved you, Cherry, and could he have expressed his last wish I know that he would have committed you as a precious charge to his mother's keeping. You are all I have left to love. Won't you love me just a little for my dead darling boy's sake?"

CHERRY—"But think of the great sorrow I have caused you, Mrs. Dean !"

MRS. DEAN—"It was your misfortune—not your fault, my child."

CHERRY (with deep feeling, but tearless)—"To-day my father will be put on trial for his life, accused of the murder of your only son—and yet you come to me, the cause of all this sorrow, with offers of sympathy and love. Oh, Mrs. Dean! you are an angel, or else you would despise and curse me." (Cherry buries her face in her hands.)

MRS. DEAN (earnestly and tenderly)—"Cherry, let me be your friend, your support, your mother and comforter, in this awful trial which has fallen upon your young life. It is time now for you to repair to the court room, where your father's trial will soon be in progress. Permit me to accompany and support you through this trying ordeal, so that the world may know, as my dead son's intended wife, how dear you are to me." (Cherry takes hands from her face and looks into Mrs. Dean's face.)

CHERRY (slowly and very earnestly. These lines must be spoken very carefully and effectively)—"And you—you, Mrs. Dean, belong to the monied aristocracy of our land! The people whom my poor father thinks are the sworn enemies of the poor; grinding us down under the iron-heel of oppression—delighting in nothing half so much as you do in the sorrow, degradation and poverty-burdened lives of your unfortunate fellow-beings! Oh, my God! how he has wronged you!"

MRS. DEAN (with much feeling)—"Never mind,

Do not think about that now. (Takes Cherry's right hand and places it on her right arm.) There, that is right, lean on me. I will support you. Courage, dear child, courage!"

[Exit left entrance Mrs. Dean and Cherry. Cherry presses handkerchief to eyes with left hand and leans on Mrs. Dean's arm. Enters right entrance Uncle Bob and Flossie. Flossie in walking costume, hat, gloves, parasol, etc. Uncle Bob very pale and harrassed.]

UNCLE BOB—"Why, baby lam', I thought you said your cousin Cherry wus hare."

FLOSSIE—"She was here, daddy, not long ago. I wonder where she has gone!"

UNCLE BOB—"We must hunt her up, fur hits time fur her to go to the court house, poor gal."

FLOSSIE—"Oh, dad, what an awful affair this is. It nearly frightens me to death. Do you think that poor uncle Mark will be hung?"

UNCLE BOB (despairingly)—"I don't know, baby lam', I don't know. Circumstances are turbly agin the pore feller, but we must hope fur the best. But come on, let's find Cherry and be off."

[Exit right entrance Uncle Bob and Flossie.]

*   *   *   *   *   *   *   *   *

[Enters left entrance Jo Black, the tramp, whom Charlie Hilton carried from the burning building. He walks feebly and tottering and looks about him.]

JO BLACK—"I don't know whose house this is—

neither do I care. The doors and windows are all
open, yet I see no one about. (Presses hand to
heart as if smitten by sudden pain—when spasm of
pain has passed.) Merciful God! Why was I rescued from the devouring flames and my sufferings
prolonged? Oh, I am so ill—so ill! (Goes to table and pours water from pitcher to goblet, drinks,
puts glass back on table.) I must rest here. I
don't care what they do with me when I am discovered. I am determined to rest now. (Sinks
down heavily on sofa—leans head back and closes
eyes—starts up wildly, presses hand to forehead.)
I wonder if this be death? My eyes grow dim. Oh,
God! I am dying! (Starts up wildly.) Oh, help!
help! I am so afraid of the awful darkness that is
falling upon me! I can not die here alone. Oh,
help! Great God, I am so afraid to die!" (Staggers around behind screen—lies down heavily on
right side, puts right hand under head, groans
aloud, then rests quietly. The screen hides his
form from persons in the room, but not from full
view of the audience.)

[Enters right entrance Uncle Bob supporting
Jennie, who is weeping bitterly.)

UNCLE BOB (seating Jennie in chair)—"Don't
give up, Jennie. Don't give up. Think of pore
Cherry and be brave fur her sake." (Jennie removes her hands from her pale face and looks up
into Uncle Bob's face.)

JENNIE (in deep anguish of spirit)—"But oh, my God, brother Bob! To think that Mark was found guilty of murder in the first degree! Oh, it will kill me—it will kill me!" (Covers face with hands and rocks body to and fro.)

UNCLE BOB (with deep emotion)—"I know it, Jennie. It looks purty bad, little woman, purty bad. But don't give up. I've got money to burn, and dog my sheep ef I don't set fire to it all to onct to git Mark outen this. 'Sides the whole EAGLE HOSE COMPANY is backen him fur all they're wurth. We'll git a new trial fur Mark, and he'll come out on top yit. Be brave now—yonder comes pore Cherry."

[Enters Cherry, supported on the right by Mrs. Dean, on the left by Charlie Hilton. Jennie gets up, meets Cherry in center, who throws herself into her mother's arms, crying in agony.)

CHERRY—"Oh, mother, mother! My poor father will die on the gallows. Oh, I would to God that I could die in his stead!"

[Uncle Bob brings chair and places it in center. Mrs. Dean walks to sofa and sits down dejectedly. Charlie Hilton walks to extreme left wing of stage and stands with folded arms, with back to audience and other figures on stage. Uncle Bob takes Cherry from her mother's arms and seats her in chair in the center.]

UNCLE BOB—"Come, come now, Cherry! This is no way to meet truble. Jist look it square in the face, same as a hunter does when a wild beast gits after him ; and like the ferocious beast it will quail and slink away. The lawyers have made an appeal fur a new trial. Your father may come out all right yit."

CHERRY (wringing her hands)—"But think of the long, weary days my father must spend in jail before he can have another trial—even if a new tria' is granted him. Oh, dear me ; dear me."

UNCLE BOB—"I know it's bad, Cherry ; but it can't be helped. Mark will be able to stand it, and you must be brave, too."

[Jo Black raises (behind the screen) himself on his elbow and listens intently. Mrs. Dean goes to Cherry's side and takes her arm.]

MRS. DEAN (tenderly)—"Come and sit beside me, poor dear child, and try to compose yourself."

[Mrs. Dean leads her to sofa, (stage business) seats herself beside Cherry, puts her arm around Cherry, who rests with her head on Mrs. Dean's shoulder. Jennie sits down beside table and rests her right arm on it—bows her head and rests it on her arm. Enters Flossie, followed by Billy Oliver. Flossie crying and wringing her hands in great anguish—her hair is in disorder, her hat hangs from her neck, held by a rubber. Billy and Charlie converse inaudibly.]

FLOSSIE—"Oh, dad, dad ! They have found poor uncle Mark guilty of murder in the first degree ! That wretched idiotic jury—the whole twelve men of them—couldn't supply brains enough

from their empty craniums to fill my little gold
thimble. And they will hang my noble uncle Mark
for the murder of Mr. Dean, when he is no more
guilty of it than I am. Oh, dad, darling dad! what
shall we do! What shall we do! (Screams as Jo
Black comes staggering into the room. Flossie
runs to her father's side.) Oh, dad! Who is this
man? It is a drunken tramp! Drive him away!
Please drive him away!"

UNCLE BOB (puts his arm around Flossie reas-
suringly)—"Don't be skeered, baby lam'. (Turns
to tramp.) Git 'out of hare! Whut do you mean
by comen into a respectable house, anyhow?"

[Jennie lifts her head, rests both elbows on table
and watches the scene.]

FLOSSIE (catching her father's arm convulsively)
—"Oh, dad! be careful, be careful—he might shoot
you."

UNCLE BOB—"Shoot nothen. (To tramp.) Move
on! Git out o'hare, I say!"

[Billy Oliver and Charlie Hilton spring forward
and each grasp an arm of Jo Black.]

BOTH TOGETHER—"Here, move on! Get out
of this house, you ragged rascal!"

[Jo Black turns an appealing look, first on Charlie, then on Billy.]

JO BLACK—"Be gentle with me, men. I am ill
—I am dying!"

UNCLE BOB—"Oh, git out ! You're drunk. Put him out, boys ; put him out."

BILLY and CHARLIE (trying to pull tramp away— "Come on, sir !"

JO BLACK—"All right. Kick me out—I'll fall down on the ground by your door and DIE LIKE A DOG. (Pulls his right arm suddenly from Charlie's grasp and shakes the forefinger of right hand menancingly.) But let me tell you—when I die A SECRET, that has a terrible bearing on the happiness of this household, DIES WITH ME ! Kick me out ! I am moneyless, homeless, friendless, ill and dying ! Do your Christian duty by me ! It will only be one more case of 'man's inhumanity to man.' But mark you—THE SECRET DIES WITH ME."

BILLY OLIVER (in a tone of amazement)—"Why, it is Jo Black ! The man you rescued from the burning building, Charlie !"

CHARLIE (in astonishment)—"It is, for a fact. (To Jo.) What are you doing in here, Jo ?"

JO BLACK—"God sent me here to save an innocent man's life from the gallows."

CHERRY (running up to the group, of which Jo Black is the central figure)—"Oh, Charlie ! What did the man say ?"

JO BLACK (looking appealingly at Cherry)— "God sent me here, Miss, in my last earthly moments to clear your father of the crime for which he has been convicted, but which I swear before high heaven he NEVER COMMITTED."

CHERRY (clasps her hands, and cries with deep emotion)—"Oh, thank God! Thank God! (Turns toward the others.) Mother, mother—Mrs. Dean— Flossie—Uncle Bob—did you all hear what the man said? MY FATHER IS INNOCENT! Thank God! Thank God!"

[All figures on the stage hasten to the group, of which Jo Black is the central figure. Jo Black gasps, (stage business) throws up his arms, staggers, as on the point of swooning. Charlie catches him in his arms.]

CHARLIE (in a voice of alarm)—"Bring a chair— get some wine—he is fainting!"

[Billy Oliver brings a chair. (Stage business.) Charlie seats Jo Black. Uncle Bob hastens to side table, pours wine from decanter, brings wine glass to Charlie, who holds it to Jo Black's lips. After Jo drinks the wine Charlie hands the glass back to Uncle Bob, who places it on the table.]

JO BLACK (revives and speaks in much stronger voice)—"Behold the man who murdered Rudolph Dean!"

UNCLE BOB—"The man must be delirious."

JO BLACK—"No, I am not delirious. I have said, and I repeat, that I and I alone, murdered Rudolph Dean!"

MRS. DEAN (clasps her hands to her heart and cries in agony)—"Oh, my noble boy! Who but a fiend could have taken his pure young life? (Grows excited and angry.) Let me kill him! Let me kill the wretch with my own hands!" (Makes a dash toward Jo Black—Uncle Bob catches and restrains her.)

UNCLE BOB (soothingly)—"Be ca'm, madam—be ca'm. I beg you, be ca'm. Let the man speak."

[Jo Black smiles faintly. Billy Oliver goes to Mrs. Dean's side, puts left arm around her, supports her, fans her with his cap. Charlie Hilton stands behind Jo Black's chair to support and administer to him.]

JO BLACK—"It is no wonder that the poor lady wants to kill me. I certainly deserve it. (Passes right hand across his forehead.) But already the dew of death is gathering upon my brow. Do not upbraid me—my time is short. Listen to my statement, which I swear (raises right hand) before God is the truth, the whole truth, and nothing but the truth. Inability to secure employment, starvation, wretchedness and despair drove me to commit the terrible crime of murder. I saw Mr. Dean when he drew fifteen hundred dollars from a bank in Greensboro on the afternoon of the murder. A mad and uncontrolable desire took possession of my heart to rob him of this sum, which would bring life, hope and youth back to my breaking heart. He was rich—he did not need the money, I told myself—while I— Oh, God only knows into what depths of despair, poverty, hunger and dirt can plunge the human soul! I dogged the young man's footsteps, watched and followed him at the midnight hour when he went alone into the lonely orchard, where his body was found. I did not intend to kill him—only to knock him down, beat him into unconsciousness and rob him. He stopped and stood leaning against a tree. I crept up behind him and dealt him a terrible blow on the head. He fell without a word or groan. I waited and listened a moment, and then attempted to rob the body. Just as I bent over it I heard swift footsteps approaching, and hastily hid myself behind a tree. Very soon the slender form of a woman was bending over the man's body, while she called him fondly by name. Then her piercing shrieks rent the still night air, and I fled wildly and undetected from the scene. A few nights later I was carried by this gentleman, (indicating Charlie) Mr. Hilton, —a brave fireman—from the basement of the Morton House, where I had been permitted to spend the night. I was suffocated with smoke, and injured besides by a piece of falling timber. But I was saved—saved for what? To be hunted and hounded from one town to another, like a wild beast of prey, to be clothed in rags and dishonor; to face starvation and despair—and in my wretchedness I cursed God for permitting my suffering to be prolonged. Ah, I know now why this was done. It was that I might make this confession and save an innocent man's life from the hangman's rope—and to save my own soul from hell. (Gasps and chokes.) Water! Air! I am suffocating! I am dying! God have mercy on my soul!"

Uncle Bob (with deep solemnity)—"Amen! Amen!"

[Jo Black leans his head half back heavily, supported by Charlie. Gasps again and is dead.]

TABLEAUX FOR CURTAIN.

Stage business. Uncle Bob stands to the right and nearest the dying man, partly bending toward him, in eager attitude, while by his side stands Jennie. Cherry sinks on her knees not far from Jo Black's chair when Uncle Bob says "Amen, amen," and remains kneeling with her face buried in her hands. Mrs. Dean leans against Billy Oliver, with her head resting on his left shoulder—he supports her with his left arm and fans her with his cap held in his right hand. When Jo Black says "I cursed God" Flossie, as if unable to hear more, runs and throws herself beside sofa and buries her face in sofa cushion. Charlie Hilton always stands at the back of Jo Black's chair, supporting the dying man's head, and doing all he can for him.

SLOW CURTAIN.

ACT SIX.

Scene—Two Years Later.

Parlor in Mark Goodwin's home—apartment better furnished than formerly.

[Enters Uncle Bob in elegant dress suit. He has been absent for two years, staying on his ranche in New Mexico. (Stage business.) Walks to mirror and surveys himself critically.]

Uncle Bob—"I wonder whut baby lam' will say to her old dad now. Jist think, she ain't seen me fur two years, and hare I am all rigged out like one of them doods I saw in Raleigh—all I lack is the cane to suck. (Feels for his trousers' pocket.) Why lookee hare; there's no pockits in these breeches! Well, I'll swan! Breeches without pockits in 'em! Jist wait till I go back to Raleigh. That snide tailor who sold me these clothes will find out that he's played a joke on the wrong man."

[Enters Flossie, a full grown young lady in elegant evening costume.]

Flossie (runs and embraces Uncle Bob)—"Oh, dear, darling old dad! I'm so glad you've come. It seems to me that I haven't seen you for twenty years. (Kisses him again and again.)

Uncle Bob (holding her off at arms length)—"Why, can this young lady, all diked out in sich fine toggery, be my little Flossie? My baby lam'?"

FLOSSIE (laughing)—"Yes, your very same baby lam', dear dad. Oh, you don't know how I have longed for you, and the sweet old days we used to have together on the ranche. You must take me home with you, now, dad; I do so long for the free wild west, and the 'round-ups,' and the 'blow-outs,' and all the fun we used to have!"

UNCLE BOB—"The round-ups! Ha, ha, ha! You'd cut a figer goen on a 'round-up' with all this toggery on, wouldn't you, now, baby lam'?"

FLOSSIE (bringing her train around with her right foot with a contemptuous sweep)—"This fine toggery, indeed! I hate it, and intend to never look at it again after we go home. But, (looking at him admiringly,) oh, dad, how swell you look."

UNCLE BOB—"Swell? Well, I should say so. I feel like I wus about to bust. But whut do you reckin, Flossie! That fool tailor in Raleigh never put no pockits in my breeches."

FLOSSIE (trying to repress a laugh)—"He didn't? Why, what a shame."

UNCLE BOB—"'Taint half as big a shame as the thrashen will be that I'll give him when I go back. You may bet your last dollar on that. (Pulls coat skirt around.) And lookee hare, he didn't put half enough stuff in my coat tail, see? They won't meet by more'n a foot."

FLOSSIE (bursts out laughing)—"Oh, that's style, daddy dear. But never mind. Just wait till we get back on the ranche and we'll dress a dummy up in this suit and put it out in the field to scare the cayotes away, eh, dad?"

UNCLE BOB—"That's jist whut we'll do, baby lam'. The dummy won't need no breeches pockits, and I reckin he won't keer if the coat tails are too narrer. But whar's your uncle Mark, an' all the folks?"

FLOSSIE—"They will all be down in a few moments, dad."

UNCLE BOB (shame-facedly)—"Flossie! I—I—I'll swan! I hate to let 'em ketch me in this hare rig. I feel so much like a fool tenderfoot looks— and dog my sheep, if I don't hate to see you draggen all that silk and lace 'round after you; and to see your purty neck and arms all bare, jist fur anybody to feast their greasy eyes on whut wants to. 'Spossen we go and git into our common-sense duds before anybody sees us, and have an old-fashion good time this evening, after we have been parted so long?"

FLOSSIE (laughing)—"All right, dad. Nothing would please me better."

UNCLE BOB (greatly relieved)—"Well, come on then, little Miss Sensible, and we'll git out of this before anybody comes." (Takes Flossie's arm.)

[Exit Uncle Bob and Flossie—Flossie smiling broadly over her shoulder at the audience. Enters Mark Goodwin and Charlie Hilton, the latter having been absent for two years—both men are in firemen's uniform.]

CHARLIE (as if continuing a conversation)—"I tell you, Captain, there is no place like home. I suffered from home-sickness the whole two years of my absence—was always longing for these familiar scenes, and the faces of the dear friends I left behind me."

MARK—"Now that we have you home again, lad, we intend to keep you here."

CHARLIE—"But, Captain, as much as I longed to be at home, I never once flattered myself that the pleasure and honor of again being a guest at your home was in store for me."

MARK—"And why not, lad? To whom should my house be open if not to the man whose loyalty and bravery resulted in saving my neck from the hangman's rope?"

CHARLIE—"But your circumstances have changed since then, Captain. Then you were a poor man and my fellow-laborer. Now you are the father of a woman who is a millionaire. I expected, such being the case, that you had grown far above me, and all your fire laddies, in fact, till I met you at the firemen's meeting to-night."

MARK (much hurt)—"Then you thought that I had turned fool, eh? Just because Mrs. Dean, in her greatness and goodness of heart, adopted my daughter Cherry as her own child, and made her

her sole heir? Oh, Charlie, Charlie! I did not think that you deemed me capable of such weakness."

CHARLIE (extending his right hand, which Mark grasps)—"Forgive me, Captain. I should have known you better than to have so misjudged you. You will forgive me, will you not?"

MARK (brushes his right hand over his eyes as if to clear them of a tearful mist)—"That's all right, Charlie."

CHARLIE—"But your daughter, Miss Cherry, will she not consider my call an intrusion—a presuming upon old acquaintanceship, and an unwarrantable liberty?"

MARK (smiling)—"She shall answer your question for herself, Charlie."

[Walks to right entrance and calls: "Cherry! will you come down to the parlor a few moments, dear?" Voice behind the scenes: "Certainly, papa!" Enters Cherry in elegant evening costume.]

CHERRY—"What is it, papa?"

MARK—"While down at a meeting of the EAGLE HOSE COMPANY this evening, Cherry, I met an old friend, and insisted upon his accompanying me home. Will you not bid him welcome?"

CHERRY—"Who is it, papa?"

MARK—"Come and see."

[Takes her arm and leads her before Charlie—who stands at table placed slightly to the right of center. Cherry looks startled for an instant, then exclaims in a voice of deep emotion.]

CHERRY—"Charlie Hilton ! Oh, Charlie, Charlie ! Thank heaven you have returned ! (Exit Mark left entrance.) Why did you leave us so abruptly, without giving us an opportunity to thank you (takes both his hands) for all you had done for us, and kept us in ignorance of your address ever since ?"

CHARLIE—"I do not deserve your kind words and this cordial welcome—indeed, I do not, Miss Cherry."

CHERRY—"You do, Charlie—indeed you do ! You deserve ten thousand times more than I am able to express. Oh, how I shudder when I think of what would have been the fate of our then wretched household had it not been for your bravery and your devotion to duty. Let me pour out my heart to you in gratitude, dearest, bravest, most loyal of men !"

CHARLIE (with great earnestness)—"Cherry—let me call you thus as in the sweet old days—listen, for I must tell you. Whatever I am my love for you has made me ! Ever since I can remember, your dear image has been my guiding star, ever inciting me to strive to live a grand, true life. If, as you say, I ever did a brave or noble deed my love for you was the motive power. This love has been my shield against the temptations which beset every young man's life ; has been my refuge in every sorrow, and the sweet companion of my weary work-a-day life ; although unrequited this love has been, still I thank God for its existence.''

CHERRY—"Charlie, have you never heard it said that true love engenders love, and will finally meet its reward?''

CHARLIE—"Yes, but Cherry, it is a rule that knows many exceptions.''

CHERRY—"There is no exception in our case, Charlie. Believe me there is not.''

CHARLIE (drops her hands)—"For the love of God, do not trifle with me !''

CHERRY—"God forbid that I should be so base. Charlie, I LOVE YOU !''

CHARLIE—"You can not mean what you say, Cherry ! It is gratitude for the service you are good enough to think I rendered you, that you have mistaken for love.''

CHERRY. (smiling archly)—"Who knows the emotions of my heart best, Charlie, you or I !''

CHARLIE—"But think of the vast difference in our social and financial positions. You are a very wealthy woman, occupying a high social position ; while I am only a mechanic and a very poor man.''

CHERRY—"I love you for your own noble self, Charlie ; and while you know that you are not my first love, my darling, you shall be my last, and my poor life,—which was almost crushed and ruined by my early sorrow,—I LAY AT YOUR FEET.''

CHARLIE (in intense rapture)—"My beloved! My own at last!" (Folds her fondly in his arms.)

UNCLE BOB (voice from behind scenes)—"Come on now, baby lam', this looks a little more like the good old times."

CHERRY (releasing herself quickly from Charlie's embrace)—"The others are coming—let us escape to the conservatory."

[Exit in haste Charlie and Cherry right entrance. Enters left entrance Uncle Bob and Flossie, dressed in costumes similar to those worn on their first appearance in the play.]

UNCLE BOB (proudly)—"Now you look like my little gal, I'll swan! I'm right down sorry fur them pore society wemin; draggen all that toggery 'round after 'em, all startched, ruffled, and laced up till they must be in misery."

FLOSSIE (laughing)—"We'll never be society folks, will we daddy dear?"

UNCLE BOB—"Dollars to doughnuts we won't, baby lam'. Give us the free wild west, with our ranches, our sheep, our cattle, our broncos——

FLOSSIE—"And our bicycles, dad!"

UNCLE BOB—"Yes, our bicycles. Oh, that reminds me—Flossie whut have you done with Billy Oliver?"

FLOSSIE—"Oh, he's here; and I love him just as much as ever."

UNCLE BOB—"Well, I'll swan! Human nater is

a curios thing. Who'd a thought that sich a sensible gal as my Flossie would have fallen in love with a tenderfoot! Has he larned to do anything else 'cept riden the bicycle and worken the type-writen machine, Flossie?"

FLOSSIE (clasping her hands enthusiastically)—"Oh, yes, dad! He has learned to play golf."

UNCLE BOB—"He's larned to do whut?"

FLOSSIE—"Play golf!"

UNCLE BOB—"Whut in the thunderation is that?"

FLOSSIE (laughing)—"We'll show you when we get home, (coaxingly) and oh, dad, you'll let poor Billy go with us, won't you?"

UNCLE BOB—"Yes, I reckin so. I want him to larn me 'bout this golf."

FLOSSIE—"I'm going to run and tell him."

UNCLE BOB—"All right. (Exit Flossie. Uncle Bob looking after her.) Well, I'll swan."

[Enters Jennie and Mark.]

UNCLE BOB—"Well, Jennie, I've had to give my gal to Billy Oliver, after all."

JENNIE (laughing)—"I told you how it would be, brother Bob; and we have just given our Cherry to Charlie Hilton."

UNCLE BOB—"Well, I'll swan. Two rich wemin marryen two poor men! Whut do you think of that, Mark?"

[Enters Flossie and Billy from left entrance. Cherry and Charlie from the right. Meet in center. Uncle Bob on left—Mark and Jennie on right.]

MARK (plainly and earnestly)—"I think, brother Bob, that it is—as it should be—a harmonious and blessed UNION OF "CAPITAL AND LABOR."

[All the figures on the stage bow low as the Curtain slowly descends.]

FINALE.

N. B.—Mark's closing speech must be with marked emphasis.

MEMBERSHIP OF THE

EAGLE HOSE CO., NO. 7,

GREENSBORO, N. C.

———:o:———

"DAUGHTER OF THE COMPANY,"

Miss Lillian Brown.

———:o:———

H. J. Elam, President.   J. W. Petty, 1st Lieut.

W. L. Cranford, Captain.   D. W. Marsh, 2nd Lieut.

E. L. Clarke, Secretary.   J. L. Thacker, Treasurer.

F. N. Taylor,	C. D. Benbow,
R. C. Whittington,	J. R. Donnell,
W. M. Adams,	L. A. Wyrick,
J. G. Fowler,	John Weatherly,
J. J. Smith,	A. L. Smith,
Wm. Smothers,	A. G. Wilson,
L. R. Thacker,	F. V. Snell,
James Gibson,	F. F. Smith,
W. L. Watson,	J. R. McClamroch,
C. B. Bogart,	W. A. Watson,
L. E. Glenn,	J. H. West,
E. K. Huff,	C. C. Shaw,

Dr. E. R. Michaux, Surgeon.

HONORARY MEMBERS.

W. E. Bevill,	J. C. Murchison,
G. W. Alley, Jr.,	R. R. King,
J. J. Nelson,	W. J. Blackburn,
C. M. Vanstory,	J. L. King,
J. M. Reece,	Neil Ellington,
A. M. Scales,	R. M. Rees,
J. H. Shaw,	C. D. Higgins.

THE EAGLE DRAMATIC CLUB.

— :o:——

President—Miss Daphne Carraway.

Vice-President—Miss Marie Wolfe.

Manager—W. H. Rees.

Lady Manager—Mrs. G. W. Whitsett.

Secretary—Miss Susie Stone.

Assistant Secretary—Miss Fodie Buie.

Treasurer—John L. Thacker.

Prompter—Miss Mamie Furgerson.

Miss Edna Vanderford, Miss M. A. Whitaker and Miss Lizzie Crocker, Musical Directors.

All members of the "Eagle Dramatic Club" are Honorary Members of the Eagle Hose Co., No. 7. There are thirty-five members in the Dramatic Club.

The regular monthly meetings of the "Eagle Dramatic Club" are held on the second Friday night of each month.

Those of the Eagle Hose Co., No. 7, are held on the first Friday night of each month. The Anniversary Meeting occurs on the first Friday night in May of each and every year.

—THE—

FIREMAN'S HEART,

AN ORIGINAL DRAMA
IN FOUR ACTS BY ......

BEATRICE MAREAN.

THRILLING, INTERESTING and REALISTIC.

Especially Adapted to Amateur Talent.

This play has been presented in many different localities, by home talent, to crowded houses, with the greatest success, for the benefit of Fire Departments.

For copies of the Drama, instructions and stage rights,   Address,

MRS. BEATRICE MAREAN,

OCALA, FLA.

LIST OF

Mrs. Beatrice Marean's

WORKS.

"THE TRAGEDIES OF OAKHURST."
"WON AT LAST."
"WHEN A WOMAN LOVES."
"HER SHADOWED LIFE."
"THE FIREMAN'S HEART."
"THE SIGN OF THE CROSS."

"Mrs. Marean's Works are the most interesting contributions to Southern literature, since the appearance of Charles Egbert Craddock's graphic tales of Tennessee Mountain life. The author is a good portrayer of human nature, and has the rare faculty of making her stories not only instructive but intensely interesting from beginning to end."--*Echoes of the South.*

Copies sent post paid on receipt of price,

CLOTH BINDING $1.12.   PAPER 31 CENTS.

Address,

MRS. BEATRICE MAREAN,

OCALA, FLA.

www.ingramcontent.com/pod-product-compliance
Lightning Source LLC
Chambersburg PA
CBHW020048030726
47499CB00007B/2641